CANADA
FOR KIDS

An Activity Book

by **SARAH SHADOWITZ**
illustrated by **ANNE WEISZ**

OVER THE FENCE PRESS

For
Joanna and Emma
and Jeremy and Simon

Text and illustration
Copyright © 1994 by Over the Fence Press
(416) 781-7081

ISBN: 1-895121-19-1

Published by
Over the Fence Press
in association with
Riverwood Publishers Ltd.
6 Donlands Avenue
P.O. Box 70
Sharon, Ontario
L0G 1V0

94 95 96 97 98 99 10 9 8 7 6 5 4 3 2 1

OTTAWA

In Ottawa, the capital city of Canada, people skate along a wide canal all winter long. Food and hot chocolate are sold at booths set up on the ice. During the day you can visit the Parliament Buildings where our federal government sits. In the summer kids enjoy seeing the changing of the guard each morning on Parliament Hill.

Find six maple leaves <u>hidden</u> in this drawing of people ice skating on the Rideau Canal.

Here are several drawings. Can you match each one to its name in both French and English?

BILINGUALISM

Canada is a bilingual country: we have two official languages–French and English. Go to a grocery store and look at some cans of vegetables or boxes of cereal and you'll see both languages written on the containers.

HOUSE

BEAVER

BOY

GIRL

HORSE

CAR

SUN

DOG

L'AUTO

LE CHEVAL

LE SOLEIL

LE CASTOR

LE GARÇON

LE CHIEN

LA MAISON

LA FILLE

Answers on last page.

ANNE OF GREEN GABLES

"Anne of Green Gables" is one of Canada's most loved characters. Lucy Maud Montgomery wrote many stories about Anne Shirley, a poor orphan girl who was adopted by an elderly brother and sister. The story is set in Prince Edward Island, Canada's smallest province.

Follow the number guide below to colour this drawing of Anne in front of Green Gables.

1 red   5 orange
2 blue   6 purple
3 pink   7 yellow
4 green   8 brown

ROCKY MOUNTAIN ANIMALS

The Canadian Rocky Mountains stretch across British Columbia and parts of Alberta and the Yukon. Skiers and hikers come from all over the world to enjoy them. Many animals live or spend time in the Rockies, including bighorn sheep, moose, grey squirrels, brown bears, Canada geese and mountain lions.

Circle the six objects which do not belong in this drawing of the Rocky Mountains. Then colour each of the animals.

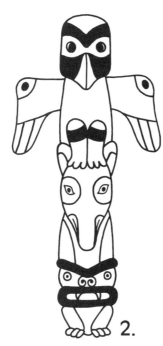

TOTEM POLES

Native artists in Canada carve and paint images of birds, animals and people onto hand-picked tree trunks, creating tall totem poles. Each totem pole tells a story. You can see totem poles in Native villages on the west coast as well as in many Canadian museums.

1.

2.

3.

4.

5.

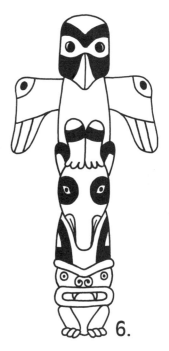

6.

Find and circle the two identical totem poles.

Answers on last page.

CANADIAN MONEY

Canadian money is unique. We call our currency "dollars", but it is different from the dollars used in the United States. We have a shiny one dollar coin, a two dollar bill and our paper money comes in many colours. The reverse side on all of our coins shows Queen Elizabeth II.

Loon
$1

Caribou
25¢

Bluenose II
10¢

Beaver
5¢

Maple Leaf
1¢

Above are drawings of the coins used in Canada. Follow the pictures below to figure out the answers to each of the arithmetic questions.

1.  = _____

2.  = _____

3.  = _____

4.  = _____

Answers on last page.

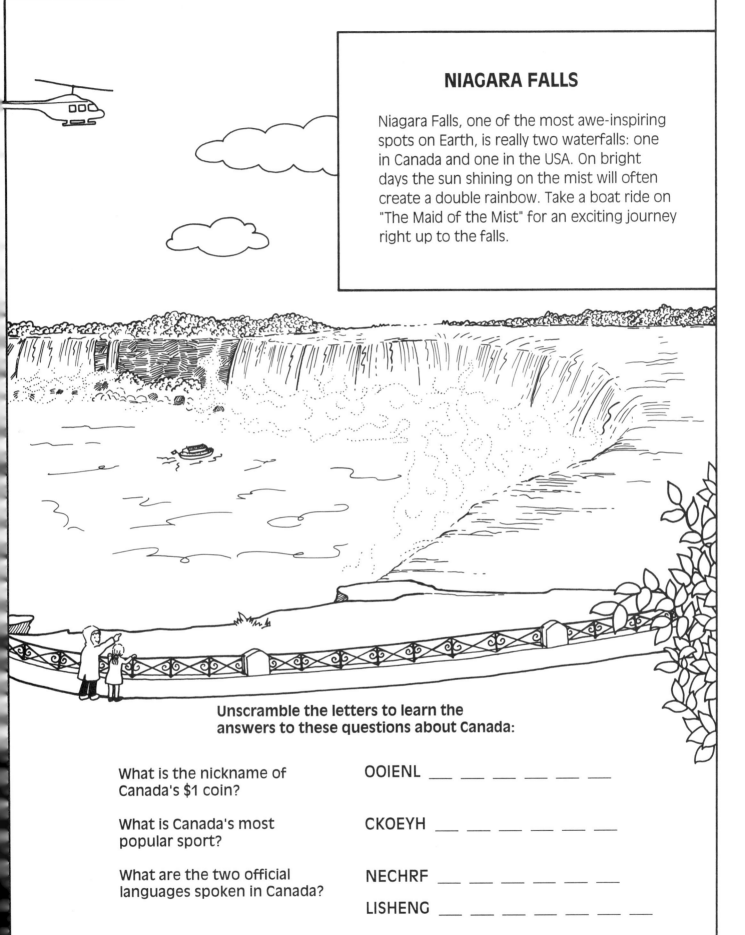

NIAGARA FALLS

Niagara Falls, one of the most awe-inspiring spots on Earth, is really two waterfalls: one in Canada and one in the USA. On bright days the sun shining on the mist will often create a double rainbow. Take a boat ride on "The Maid of the Mist" for an exciting journey right up to the falls.

Unscramble the letters to learn the answers to these questions about Canada:

What is the nickname of Canada's $1 coin?

OOIENL __ __ __ __ __ __

What is Canada's most popular sport?

CKOEYH __ __ __ __ __ __

What are the two official languages spoken in Canada?

NECHRF __ __ __ __ __ __

LISHENG __ __ __ __ __ __ __

Answers on last page.

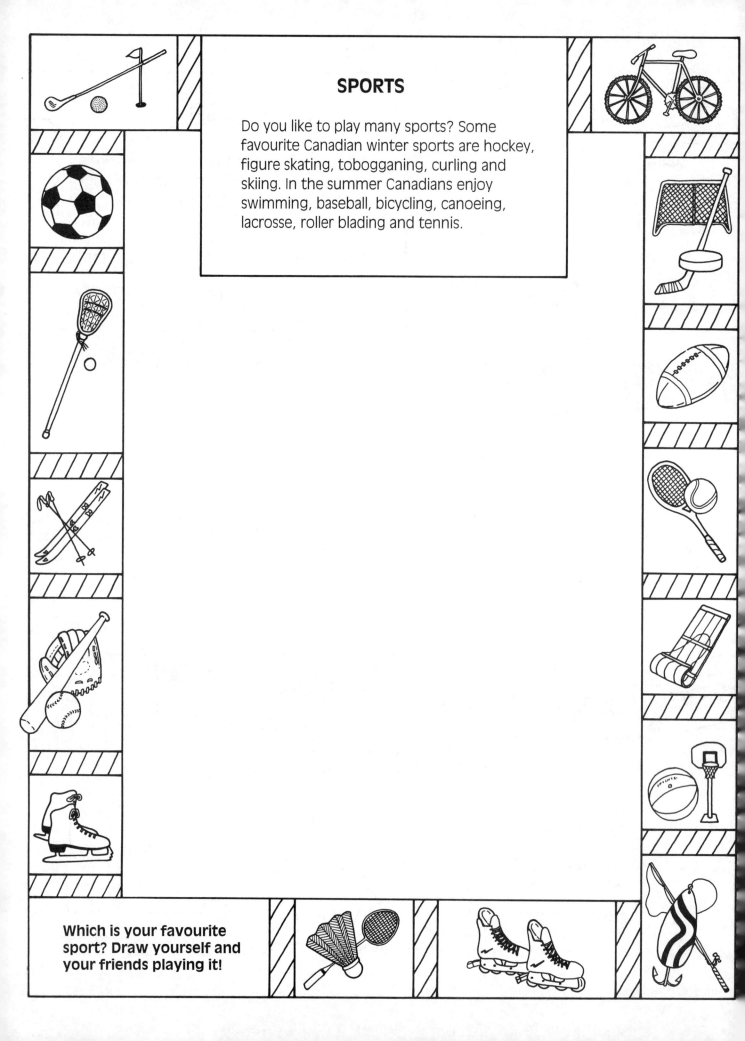

SPORTS

Do you like to play many sports? Some favourite Canadian winter sports are hockey, figure skating, tobogganing, curling and skiing. In the summer Canadians enjoy swimming, baseball, bicycling, canoeing, lacrosse, roller blading and tennis.

Which is your favourite sport? Draw yourself and your friends playing it!

THE INUIT

The Inuit people live in the Arctic areas of Canada, where it is cold much of the year. Many Inuit live in igloos in winter and tents in summer, while others live in homes much like those in southern Canada. The Inuit used to be called "Eskimos", but now most Canadians refer to them by their own name, "Inuit", which means "the people".

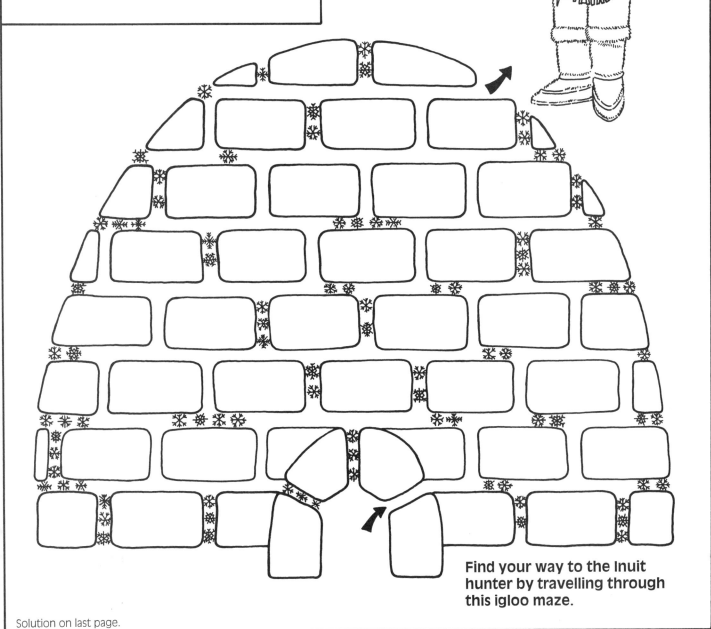

Find your way to the Inuit hunter by travelling through this igloo maze.

Solution on last page.

THE GOLD RUSH

The famous Klondike Gold Rush of 1898 took place in one of Canada's territories–The Yukon. People from all over the world hurried to the Yukon to pan for gold, hoping that they could "get rich quick". You can read about the Yukon's Gold Rush in books by Pierre Berton and Jack London.

Can you name four other metals besides gold?

Find and circle eight Canada geese hidden in this picture.

Answers on last page.

CANADIAN CITIES

In every large Canadian city kids can find lots of exciting activities. In Vancouver you can take a ferry ride; in Toronto, explore the Ontario Science Centre. Experience the Biodome in Montreal; or visit a children's museum in Winnipeg. Halifax, Fredericton, St. John's, Saskatoon, Dawson City and Charlottetown are some of the Canadian cities which kids enjoy visiting.

To find out the unusual names of four Canadian cities, look at the picture above each box and name it. Then print its first letter in the box.

1.

2.

3.

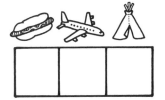

4.

Answers on last page.

TERRY FOX

Terry Fox was a very determined young man. When he was a teenager, doctors found cancer just below the knee in his right leg and his leg had to be removed. To raise money to help find a cure for cancer, Terry began a run from Newfoundland to British Columbia, wearing an artificial leg. But near Thunder Bay, Ontario he became sick again and had to end his "Marathon of Hope". Terry died soon after, but his hope lives on. The research continues, thanks in part to the millions of dollars raised through Terry Fox Runs held every year.

Copy the black parts in the squares below onto the larger squares having the same number and letter. Then you will see Terry Fox on his Marathon of Hope. We have done boxes C2 and B3 for you.

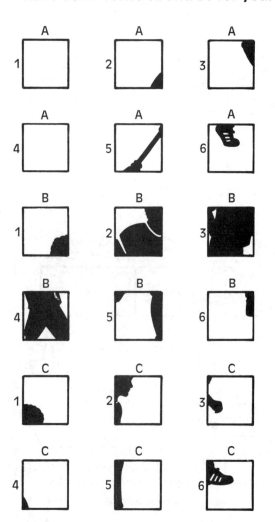

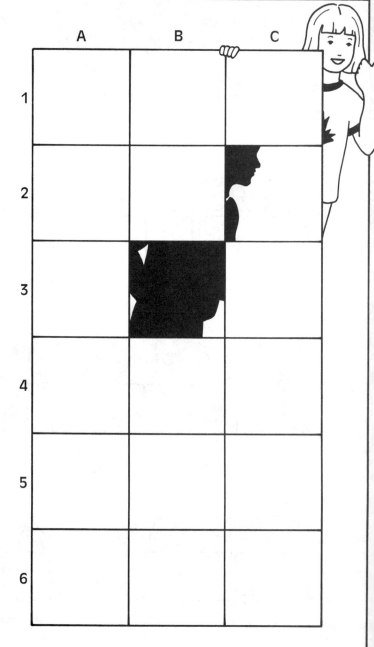

Solution on last page.

PIONEER DAYS

When Europeans came to Canada many years ago, they had to build their own homes. Often they cut down trees to make a clearing and then they built houses and farmed the land in order to survive. Pioneer families had to do everything themselves: sew clothing, grow food, milk cows, churn butter and even make soap. Children had important chores to do, also, such as gathering eggs and firewood and feeding the animals.

Help these pioneers find their way through the woods to their homestead.

Solution on last page.

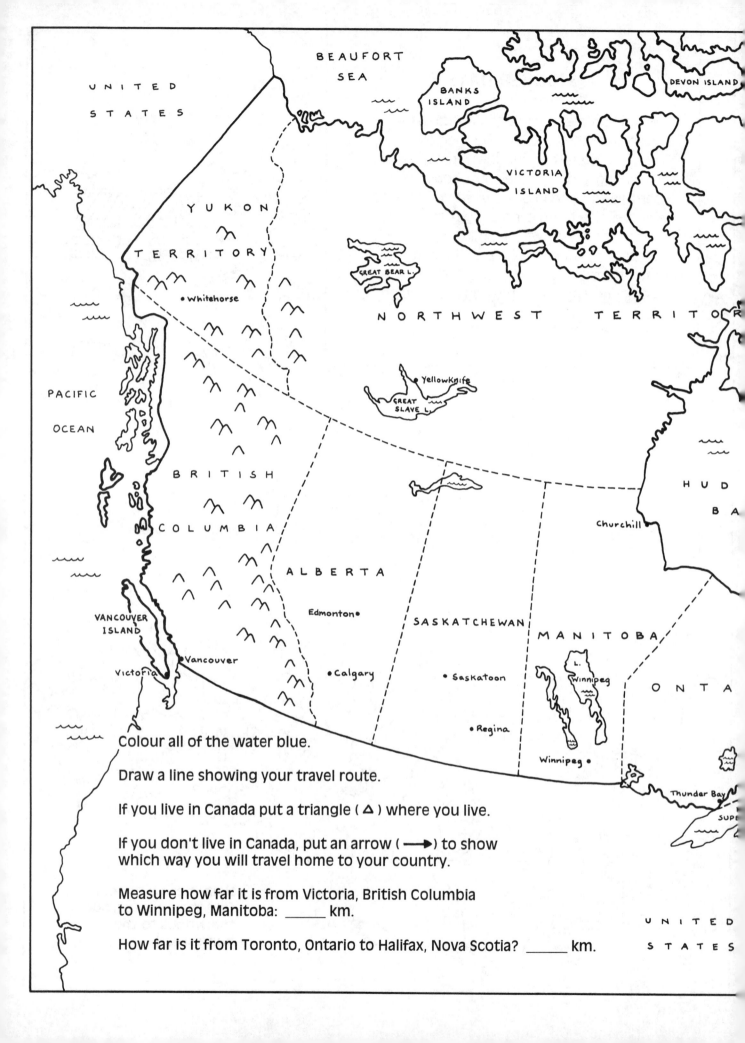

BEAUFORT
SEA

UNITED
STATES

BANKS
ISLAND

DEVON ISLAND

VICTORIA
ISLAND

Y U K O N

T E R R I T O R Y

GREAT BEAR L.

• Whitehorse

N O R T H W E S T   T E R R I T O R

PACIFIC

OCEAN

• YellowKnife

GREAT
SLAVE L.

HUD

BA

B R I T I S H

Churchill •

C O L U M B I A

A L B E R T A

VANCOUVER
ISLAND

Edmonton •

S A S K A T C H E W A N

M A N I T O B A

O N T A

Vancouver •

• Calgary

• Saskatoon

L.
Winnipeg

Victoria •

• Regina

Winnipeg •

Colour all of the water blue.

Draw a line showing your travel route.

Thunder Bay

SUPE

If you live in Canada put a triangle (△) where you live.

If you don't live in Canada, put an arrow (⟶) to show
which way you will travel home to your country.

Measure how far it is from Victoria, British Columbia
to Winnipeg, Manitoba: _____ km.

UNITED

How far is it from Toronto, Ontario to Halifax, Nova Scotia? _____ km.

STATES

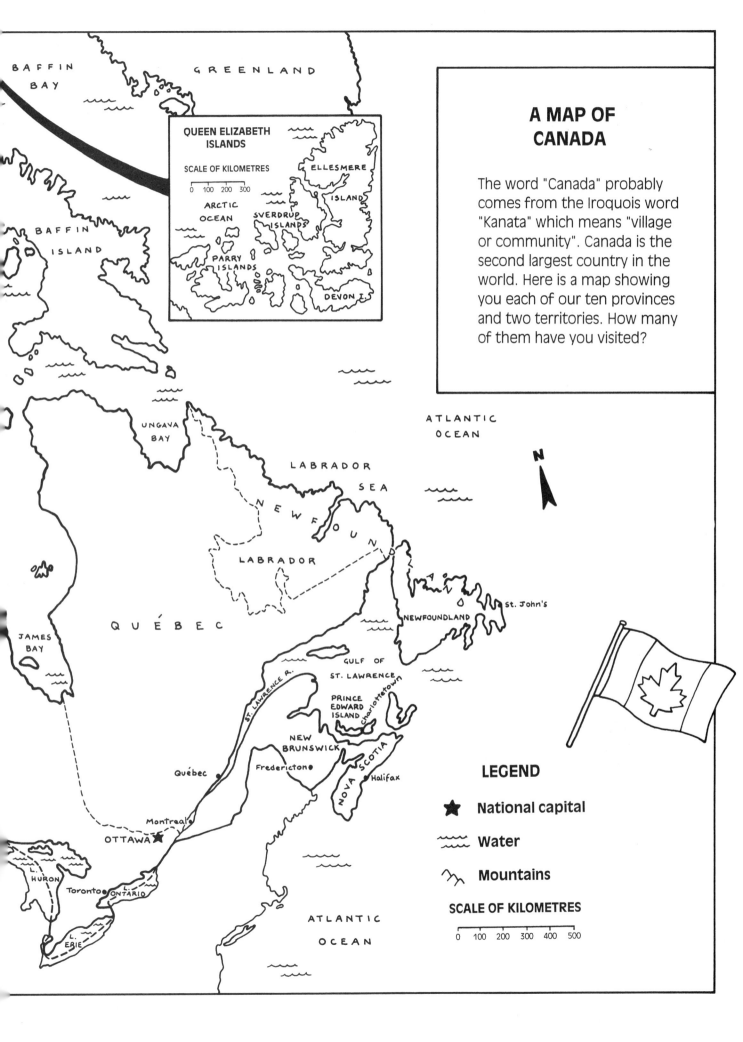

BAFFIN
BAY

GREENLAND

**QUEEN ELIZABETH
ISLANDS**

SCALE OF KILOMETRES

0   100 200 300

ELLESMERE
ISLAND

ARCTIC
OCEAN

SVERDRUP
ISLANDS

BAFFIN
ISLAND

PARRY
ISLANDS

DEVON I.

A MAP OF
CANADA

The word "Canada" probably
comes from the Iroquois word
"Kanata" which means "village
or community". Canada is the
second largest country in the
world. Here is a map showing
you each of our ten provinces
and two territories. How many
of them have you visited?

ATLANTIC
OCEAN

N

UNGAVA
BAY

LABRADOR

SEA

NEWFOUN

LABRADOR

St. John's

NEWFOUNDLAND

QUÉBEC

JAMES
BAY

GULF OF
ST. LAWRENCE

ST. LAWRENCE R.

PRINCE
EDWARD
ISLAND

Charlottetown

NEW
BRUNSWICK

Québec

Fredericton

NOVA SCOTIA

Halifax

Montreal

OTTAWA ★

LEGEND

★ **National capital**

〜〜〜 **Water**

⌃⌃⌃ **Mountains**

Toronto

L. ONTARIO

L.
HURON

L.
ERIE

ATLANTIC

OCEAN

SCALE OF KILOMETRES

0   100 200 300 400 500

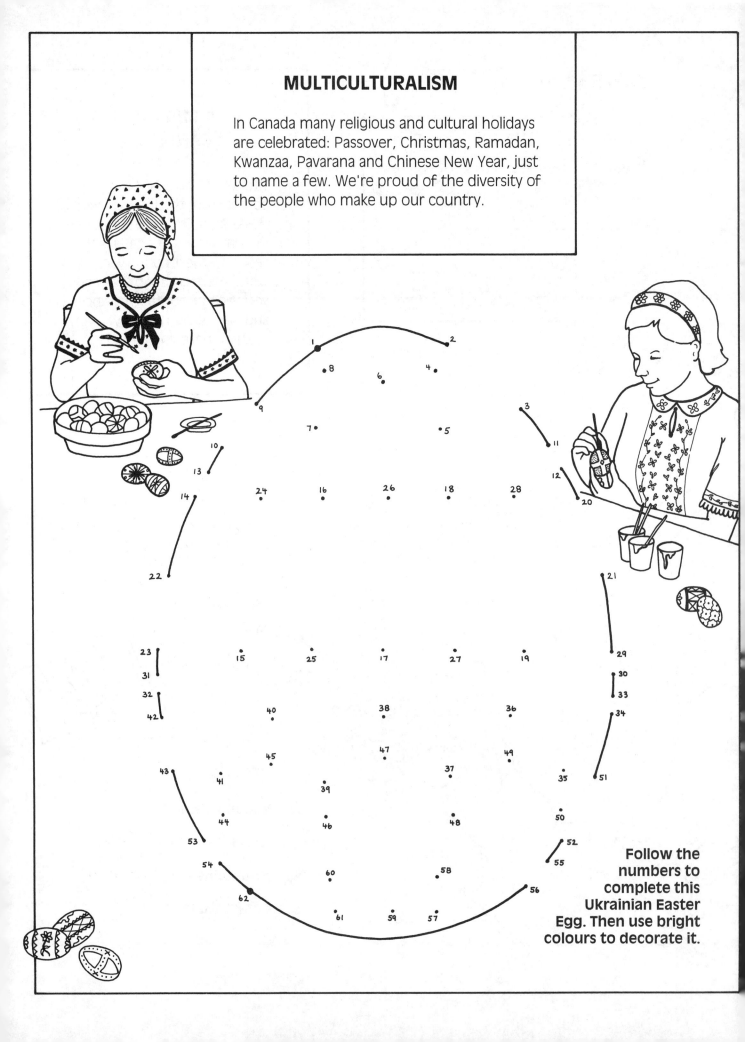

MULTICULTURALISM

In Canada many religious and cultural holidays are celebrated: Passover, Christmas, Ramadan, Kwanzaa, Pavarana and Chinese New Year, just to name a few. We're proud of the diversity of the people who make up our country.

Follow the numbers to complete this Ukrainian Easter Egg. Then use bright colours to decorate it.

MAPLE SYRUP

Canada is famous for its forests. Our maple trees produce maple sap every year. In late winter you can participate in the fun of "sugaring-off" and watch sap being taken from maple trees and then boiled in large vats to turn it into sweet maple syrup.

Colour this drawing of sugaring-off by following the key below.

1 red   5 grey
2 blue   6 orange
3 pink   7 purple
4 green   8 brown

SNOW

In parts of Canada snow falls all through the winter. There are over a dozen words in the Inuit language for snow, each describing a different "type" of snow. Wet sloppy snow, for example, is called <u>missalerak</u> and deep soft snow is known as <u>mauja</u>.

Here are half drawings of four snowflakes. The other sides are the same, or "symmetrical". See if you can finish them yourself!

THE MENNONITES

Have you ever baked bread "from scratch"? In central Canada a group of farmers known as Old Order Mennonites still lives the lifestyle of the pioneers–baking bread and using horses instead of cars. The Mennonites live as a community in the country rather than in cities.

Please organize these pictures of bread making to put them in their correct order:

B ___ ___ ___ ___

Answers on last page.

PREHISTORIC CANADA

In Alberta, Manitoba and Saskatchewan, the prairie provinces, you can visit the plains on which dinosaurs lived millions of years ago. At the Calgary Zoo there are huge outdoor make-believe dinosaurs for kids to see. And in Drumheller, Alberta you can visit the Royal Tyrrell Museum of Paleontology and then drive along the "Dinosaur Trail".

BRONTOSAURUS

STEGOSAURUS

ALLOSAURUS

Connect the dots to complete the dinosaur.

A CANADIAN ASTRONAUT

Dr. Roberta Bondar, Canada's first woman astronaut, was a crew member on the Discovery Shuttle, a space ship which circled Earth in January, 1992. She was able to see what our planet looked like from outer space, and she described it as a "bright, shiny jewel".

Help Dr. Bondar find her way back to Earth through this planetary maze.

Solution on last page.

BOATS IN CANADA

Here are several Canadian boats. You can see the HMS Nonsuch, a wooden ketch, in Winnipeg at the "Manitoba Museum of Man and Nature". The Bluenose II, a schooner, sails out of Halifax, Nova Scotia. You'll find ferryboats, canoes and fishing boats all over our country, while kayaks are used mostly in the Yukon and Northwest Territories.

1. ___ ___ ___ ___ ___ ___ ___ ___ ___ ___
   5   18   4   7   21   7   4   14   6   5

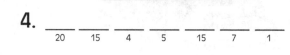

4. ___ ___ ___ ___ ___ ___ ___
   20   15   4   5   15   7   1

   ___ ___ ___ ___
   16   21   10   17

2. ___ ___ ___ ___ ___ ___ ___ ___ ___
   20   9   8   8   19   16   21   10   17

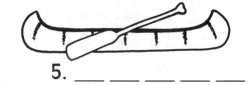

5. ___ ___ ___ ___ ___
   6   10   7   21   9

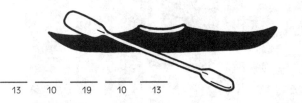

3. ___ ___ ___ ___ ___
   13   10   19   10   13

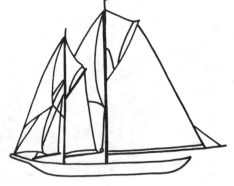

6. ___ ___ ___ ___ ___ ___ ___ ___ ___ ___
   16   3   14   9   7   21   4   9   15   15

1	G	8	R	15	I
2	D	9	E	16	B
3	L	10	A	17	T
4	S	11	J	18	M
5	H	12	V	19	Y
6	C	13	K	20	F
7	N	14	U	21	O

Follow the code to discover the name of each of these boats.

QUÉBEC CITY

Québec City, the oldest city in North America, was built hundreds of years ago by French settlers. Placed high on top of a hill above the St. Lawrence River, it was surrounded by a thick wall in order to protect the small French colony from attack. The wall around the city still stands today.

Here are two drawings of the Québec City skyline. Find and circle the twelve differences between the drawings.

Solution on last page.

THE ARCTIC

The Arctic lands of Canada are a vast, beautiful expanse still largely untouched by people. The sun never sets above the Arctic Circle on June 21st, the longest day of the year! And later, at the end of each summer, the world-famous northern lights (known as the Aurora Borealis) create shimmering, colourful displays of light in the night sky.

Colour in the shapes with dots to find these Arctic animals: seal, Arctic fox, walrus, polar bear, whale, caribou and snowy owl.

1.

2.

THE RCMP

The Royal Canadian Mounted Police (RCMP), first formed in Saskatchewan in the 1870s, are known all over the world as the law-enforcement officers of our federal government. They also protect some of our provinces. To many people, the bright scarlet and black uniforms of the RCMP are a symbol of Canada.

3.

4.

5.

6.

Find the two identical RCMP officers in this drawing. Then colour all of the outfits red and brown. The RCMP hats should be coloured tan.

Answers on last page.

OUR OCEANS AND LAKES

Canada is bordered by water in almost every direction: the Atlantic Ocean to the east, the Pacific Ocean to the west, the Arctic Ocean to the north and the Great Lakes along part of our southern border. The animals and fish which live in the water play an important role in the balance of nature.

Connect these water animals to their names. Then colour the drawing using crayons or markers.

LOBSTER   SALMON   WHALE   SEAL   CLAM   WALRUS   BEAVER   DUCK

Which path will lead this cowboy safely back to the corral?

THE CALGARY STAMPEDE

Cowboys are a part of the history of Canada's west. Each year in cities throughout our western provinces you'll find exciting rodeos with bucking broncos, calf roping and chuck-wagon races. The Calgary Stampede is the largest rodeo in Canada.

Solution on last page.

THE CANADA FOR KIDS'
TRAVEL DIARY

Fill out this Travel Diary when you go on a vacation in Canada so that you'll always remember your special trip!

My name _____

Date_____

WHERE I LIVE

My address_____

_____

_____

My phone number_____

My school_____

A DRAWING OF MY FAMILY ON VACATION

WHAT I DID ON MY TRIP

_____

_____

_____

_____

_____

HOW WE TRAVELLED

Draw five other modes of transportation which you used on your trip.

PLACES I VISITED

_____

_____

_____

_____

_____

ANIMALS I SAW

_____

_____

_____

_____

_____

ANSWERS AND SOLUTIONS

Bilingualism
House – la maison; beaver – le castor;
boy – le garçon; girl – la fille; horse – le cheval;
car – l'auto; sun – le soleil; dog – le chien.

Totem Poles
Numbers 1 and 6 are identical.

Canadian Money
1. $1.16,   2. 55 cents,   3. 8 cents,   4. $2.30.

Niagara Falls
Loonie, hockey, French, English.

The Gold Rush
Silver, copper, nickel, tin, lead, iron, platinum, aluminum.

Canadian Cities
1. Moose Jaw (Saskatchewan), 2. Ha Ha Bay (Newfoundland),
3. Medicine Hat (Alberta), 4. Flin Flon (Manitoba).

The Mennonites
B, E, C, A, D.

Boats in Canada
1. HMS Nonsuch 2. Ferryboat 3. Kayak
4. Fishing boat 5. Canoe 6. Bluenose II.

The RCMP
Numbers 2 and 3 are identical.

The Inuit
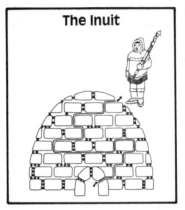

Pioneer Days

A Canadian Astronaut
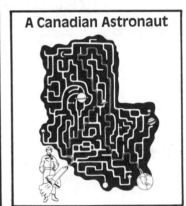

The Calgary Stampede
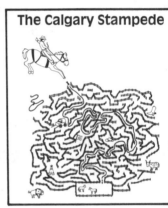

Terry Fox

Québec City
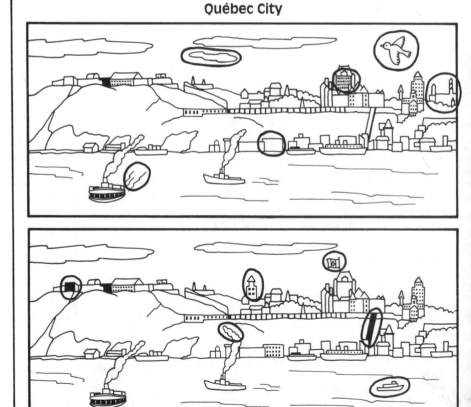